THE
MIDDLE
SHEEP

Extraordinary Ernie
& Marvelous Maud

THE MIDDLE SHEEP

Frances Watts
Illustrated by Judy Watson

Eerdmans Books for Young Readers

Grand Rapids, Michigan / Cambridge, U.K.

Text © 2008 Frances Watts
Illustrations © 2008 Judy Watson

First published 2008 in Australia by
Australian Broadcasting Corporation

This edition published 2010 in the United States of America by
Eerdmans Books for Young Readers
an imprint of Wm. B. Eerdmans Publishing Co.

Wm. B. Eerdmans Publishing Co.
2140 Oak Industrial Dr. NE, Grand Rapids, Michigan 49505
P.O. Box 163, Cambridge CB3 9PU U.K.

www.eerdmans.com/youngreaders

Manufactured at Versa Press, East Peoria, Illinois, USA,
in June 2010; first printing

10 11 12 13 14 15 16   7 6 5 4 3 2 1

Library of Congress Cataloging-in-Publication Data

Watts, Frances.
The middle sheep / by Frances Watts; illustrated by Judy Watson.
p. cm. — (Extraordinary Ernie & Marvelous Maud; bk. 2)
Summary: When Maud becomes gloomy about being a "middle sheep,"
she decides that as Extraordinary Ernie's sidekick, she deserves a
sidekick too, which makes Ernie, an only child, feel left out,
leading to bickering between the two of them.
ISBN 978-0-8028-5368-4 (alk. paper)
[1. Superheroes — Fiction. 2. Sheep — Fiction. 3. Birth order — Fiction.
4. Cooperativeness — Fiction.] I. Watson, Judy, 1959- ill. II. Title.
PZ7.W3355Mi 2010
[Fic] — dc22
2010010936

For my very cute (and smart)
little sister, Stephanie
— *F.W.*

For our Middle Pete
— *J.W.*

ONE

Ernie Eggers stood outside the Superheroes Society (Baxter Branch) on Main Street, waiting. Maud was late.

Because he was a newish superhero — he had only been in training for a few months, after all — it still gave him a thrill to see himself in costume. Angling himself slightly so as to see his reflection in the window of the laundromat next door, he admired the fluorescent green one-piece suit with the gold lightning bolts on the sleeves and the long, swishing cape.

Finally he heard the familiar *clip-clop* of hooves

tripping down the pavement and saw his sidekick, pink cape fluttering, trotting toward him.

Ernie had been thrilled to win a superhero contest and become Extraordinary Ernie (after school on Mondays, Tuesdays, and Thursdays, and all day Saturday). But his excitement had turned to dismay when he discovered that his sidekick was to be a sheep. It didn't take him long to realize, though, that there had never been another sheep quite like Marvelous Maud.

"I'm sorry I'm late," panted Maud.

"That's all right," said Ernie. "Is everything okay?"

"Don't ask!" said Maud, throwing a leg in the air. "I don't want to talk about it."

"Oh, sorry," said Ernie, bewildered.

"Well, if you must know," Maud continued, as if she hadn't heard him, "it's all my little sister's fault."

The pair began to walk up Main Street on their regular Saturday patrol, which stretched along the block of shops from the Baxter town hall at one end to the park at the other.

"I was getting ready this morning and I couldn't find my superhero cape anywhere. And do you know where it was?"

Ernie, who didn't know, shook his head.

"My little sister was using it for dress-up!" Maud said in disgust. "She has no respect for my things."

Ernie grimaced sympathetically.

"Do you have any brothers or sisters?" Maud asked.

"No," said Ernie. "I'm an only child."

"Oh, you don't know how lucky you are," she sighed. "I'm a middle sheep. I've got an older sister and a younger sister, and next to them I might as well be invisible."

Ernie found this hard to believe.

"I'm not smart, like my big sister Doris." She sniffed.

"But Maud," Ernie protested, "you're the smartest person — or sheep — I know."

Maud shot him a grateful look. "And you'd say I was cute, wouldn't you, Ernie? Well, apparently I'm not as cute as my little sister Mavis," Maud grumbled before Ernie could respond.

"Don't be upset, Maud," said Ernie earnestly. "I mean, look at you — you're a superhero sidekick. You stamp out mischief and run down wrongdoers. No sheep has ever contributed so much to society!"

Maud brightened. "You're right," she said. Maud's natural good cheer was never far from the surface.

They had a busy morning. Saturday was always bustling.

Ernie found Mrs. Evans's lost purse, which she had dropped into a pile of bananas in the supermarket.

Maud gave a screaming child a ride on her back until he was all smiles.

When a sudden gust of wind blew Mr. Carter's toupee from his head, Ernie chased it all the way down the street.

And just before lunchtime, Maud threw herself in front of a runaway stroller, earning the praise of the thankful mother.

They stopped for lunch, taking some cucumber

sandwiches to the park as usual. (Ernie didn't eat meat when in the company of Maud, who was a vegetarian.)

As they lazed under a tree, soaking up the few rays of late-summer sunshine, Maud said thoughtfully, "I was thinking about what you said this morning — about making a contribution to society. And it's true that as a superhero sidekick I've been able to help people. But it's also helped me so much, too. I'm seeing a lot more of the world, making new friends . . . It's a shame that more middle sheep haven't had the opportunity I've had."

"I know what you mean, Maud," said Ernie. Together they gathered up their trash and dropped it in the can on their way back to Main Street.

As they left the park they were surprised to see that a crowd had formed around the tree that stood near the supermarket.

All the faces were tilted up, looking at something in the branches.

At that moment one of the crowd noticed the approaching superheroes. "Come quick!" he cried. "There's a poor little kitten stuck in the tree!"

Oh no! Ernie and Maud began to run.

TWO

The crowd moved back when the two superheroes reached the tree so they could see for themselves the mewling black kitten stuck high in the branches.

Ernie and Maud looked at each other.

"I'll have to climb up and get it, Maud," Ernie said seriously.

The sheep nodded her agreement. "I'll give you a boost," she said. "And Ernie? Be careful."

Maud braced herself, and Ernie stepped onto her broad back, from which he could reach the tree's lowest branch. Seizing it, he swung himself

up and from there began to scale the trunk. His mouth felt dry and he tried hard not to look down.

About halfway up his foot slipped on some crumbling bark.

"Oooh!" gasped the crowd.

Ernie's heart pounded as he scrabbled for a foothold, desperately gripping the nearest branch. After what seemed like an age swinging high above the ground, his left foot finally found a sturdy knot.

"Aaah!" the crowd breathed in relief.

Ernie waited till his heart was beating normally again, then continued to climb.

When at last he reached the branch that held the whimpering kitten he sat down and paused to steady himself. Then with a quick movement he grabbed hold of the frightened animal. It squirmed and struggled in his grasp, but he took the end of his cape, pulled it over his shoulder and wrapped the kitten securely. Clasping the bundle of kitten to his chest, he began the climb down, a move made more difficult by the fact that he only

had the use of one arm.
When he still had several
yards to go, the kitten gave
an ear-splitting yowl and flew from
Ernie's hold, causing him to wobble dangerously.

Luckily, Maud was on the alert. She trotted back and forth, trying to position herself beneath the falling kitten, who landed in a bed of springy white curls.

By the time a shaky Ernie reached the ground, Maud and the kitten appeared to be deep in conversation, though Ernie couldn't make out what was being said.

The crowd, who had cheered the kitten's rescue, drifted away, leaving the two superheroes and the kitten alone.

"What kind of a crazy . . ." Ernie began.

Maud, who had been nodding as she listened to the cat's story, took him aside. "Tabby is a middle kitten," she explained, "and she was fed up with being ignored. That's why she ran up the tree. Anyway, I've just been telling her how much being your sidekick has helped me, and it's given me a great idea. Tabby can be my sidekick!"

"I've never heard of a sidekick having a sidekick," Ernie objected.

"True, but then you'd never heard of having a sheep for a sidekick either, and look how well that's turned out," Maud argued.

Ernie shrugged. He was learning that it was useless trying to talk Maud out of anything once she'd set her mind to it. He looked at his watch. "Look at the time," he said in surprise. "We'd better get back to base to make our report."

❁

Back at 32 Main Street, the four original members of the Superheroes Society (Baxter Branch) awaited their newest recruits. Housecat Woman was asleep in the armchair as usual, but the others were gathered around the table where Super Whiz, president and brains of the Baxter Branch, was lecturing them on "Superheroism in the New Millennium."

In recognition of Baxter's record-low levels of mischief, Super Whiz had been invited to give a lecture at the National Superheroes Conference the following month, and he'd insisted on trying out several possible topics on his colleagues. Valiant Vera — who was the bravest and fastest

of the superheroes and also, Ernie had decided, a very nice person — was politely trying to look interested.

Amazing Desmond, yawning loudly, wasn't even bothering to try. It was Amazing Desmond who had first spotted Ernie's superhero potential and Maud's sidekick potential — and although he was the least serious superhero you could possibly imagine, both Ernie and Maud agreed that Desmond was indeed amazing.

When Ernie and Maud pushed open the shabby brown door of the anonymous storefront, Desmond leapt eagerly to his feet to greet them. Ernie wondered at first why Desmond seemed so pleased to see them, until he noticed the thick wad of papers in Super Whiz's hand.

"Ah, you're just in time to hear the end of my new lecture," said Super Whiz. Valiant Vera gave them a weary smile.

"Oh. . . ah, I think I'm

expected at home," said Ernie quickly. "Aren't you, Maud?"

Maud could only give a muffled bleat, as she had the scruff of a kitten's neck held carefully between her teeth. Placing Tabby gently on the floor, Maud said, "Look! I've got a sidekick!" Before she could explain, there was a loud hiss. Housecat Woman had sprung from her armchair and retreated into the corner, eyeing the kitten suspiciously.

The kitten was not a success. Ernie was amazed that so much chaos could be caused by such a small bundle of fur.

First, Tabby pranced over to Valiant Vera.

"What a dear little kitten!" cooed Vera as Tabby rolled onto her back to show a soft white belly. But when Vera leaned down to tickle Tabby's tummy her hand was attacked by tooth and claw. "Little wretch!" cried Vera, snatching back her hand and glaring at the kitten.

Next it attacked Ernie's cape. The faster he twisted and turned, trying to shake it off, the deeper it sank its claws into the shiny green fabric.

Frustrated, Ernie took his cape in both hands and yanked it, sending the kitten tumbling onto the floor. "I should have left you in the tree," he muttered angrily.

Just then Amazing Desmond sneezed twelve times in a row. Pulling an enormous spotted handkerchief from the waistband of his tights, he honked into it loudly. "Allergic to cats," he wheezed.

Finally, Tabby sprang onto the table. She rolled and skidded along the polished wooden surface, knocking over a glass of water. It spilled all over Super Whiz's lecture.

Super Whiz turned a peculiar shade of purple, as if he were about to burst.

It was the last straw.

"I'm sorry, Maud," Valiant Vera said firmly. "I'm afraid that Tabby will have to go."

THREE

Despite the problems with her first sidekick, Maud was determined.

On Monday afternoons Super Whiz held the regular weekly superhero training session. This consisted of Super Whiz giving speeches on things like "Capes: Dry-clean or Gentle Machine Wash?" and "Should Superheroes Wear Sunhats?" When Maud turned up at the Superheroes Society office the next week, Ernie was surprised to see a little brown rabbit follow her into the room.

"This is Albert," Maud said. "He's a middle bunny."

Desmond pulled out his hankie. Vera shook her head and pointed toward the door.

On Tuesday afternoon, Ernie and Maud patrolled Main Street.

"Slow down, Ernie," Maud begged. "Poor Harold can't keep up."

Ernie turned to watch the progress of Harold, a friendly but slow-moving tortoise — a middle tortoise, of course.

"I'm practically walking in place already,"

Ernie complained.

"Give Harold a chance," Maud chided. "It's his first time on patrol."

"And at this rate, Harold's first patrol will last for *years*," Ernie said under his breath.

After an hour in which they still hadn't walked an entire block of Main Street, Maud agreed that maybe a tortoise wasn't the ideal sidekick.

On Thursday Maud was accompanied by a middle horse. Ernie was sure he could hear someone softly singing, "Extraordinary Ernie had a Farm" as the three of them walked — and clopped — down Main Street.

On Saturday Valiant Vera asked Ernie and Maud to spend some of the morning patrolling the park. This was usually one of Ernie's favorite patrols. He and Maud would amble along the paths around the pond, talking about this and that. But today conversation was impossible.

"What?" said Ernie as Maud mumbled something. "Golfing needs a heavy book? What does *that* mean?"

She mumbled louder.

"Maud," said Ernie, a little impatiently, "put the goldfish down."

Maud gently lowered the plastic bag of water, in which Herbert the goldfish was swimming, to the ground. "I was just telling you that goldfish are heavier than they look."

Ernie was unsympathetic.

"How would you like to be the middle fish of seven brothers and sisters?" Maud wanted to know. Ernie had to admit that he wouldn't like it very much at all.

But having a sidekick who couldn't talk because she was carrying a goldfish in her mouth was not much use.

He felt a bit guilty when Herbert blinked his big sad goldfish eyes in disappointment, but as Maud returned Herbert to the pond where he lived, Ernie told himself it was for the best.

The following week, Maud didn't dare bring a sidekick to Super Whiz's Monday afternoon class, but on Tuesday she was trailed by a duckling ("too skittery") and on Thursday she brought along a middle mouse. At least she thought she had. But, though she and Ernie looked and looked, they couldn't see Tiny anywhere.

That Saturday, to Ernie's relief, Maud announced that she wasn't going to bring any more sidekicks on patrol.

"Don't think I'm giving up on the idea, Ernie," she warned him. "I still want to give opportunities to deserving middle animals. But I've learned this week that not just any sidekick will do."

Sticking her nose into her fleecy front, she pulled out a flyer, which she handed to Ernie.

"'Marvelous Maud's Superhero Sidekick Try-outs. Next Sunday in Mackie's Meadow. Middle Animals Only,'" he read. "Um, great idea," he told her. But secretly Ernie wasn't so sure. The truth was, he had been feeling left out the past two weeks. Maud had been having a wonderful time with her sidekicks, comparing notes on their brothers' and sisters' annoying habits. Being an only child, Ernie was never included in the conversation.

Not only that, while Ernie would be the first to admit that Maud was a wonderful sidekick, to be accompanied on patrol by two animals didn't seem quite right for a superhero.

And, more than anything, Ernie missed Maud and the feeling that the two of them were a team. It seemed to him that being his sidekick just wasn't important to her anymore.

FOUR

The following Saturday, Maud was late again. When it seemed like she was never going to arrive, Ernie began the patrol on his own.

He had been patrolling alone for almost an hour when Maud finally galloped up Main Street to join him. Her fleece was uncombed and her cape was crumpled.

"Super Whiz recommends that you use a warm iron after a cape comes out of the washing machine," Ernie reminded her.

Maud turned toward him with a face like thunder. "My cape hasn't been in the washing machine," she said furiously. "You know I always dry-clean."

"Maud," said Ernie, surprised by her anger, "what's wrong?"

"Mavis!" growled the sheep. Several hours passed before she said another word.

In fact, Maud's bad mood lasted the rest of the morning. Whenever Ernie tried to strike up a conversation, she would give a wordless bleat that sounded remarkably like a grunt. She wouldn't even be drawn into guessing which of the thirteen lectures Super Whiz had prepared so far would be the one he gave at the National Conference.

Finally, Ernie gave up. His own mood had been growing worse and worse. What good was a sidekick who was always late and always cranky? he grumbled to himself.

At lunchtime, they took their cucumber sandwiches to the park as usual, but neither of them headed for their usual spot under the tree. Ernie took his sandwich to the bench by the pond, while Maud stalked over to a patch of grass at the far side of the park.

After lunch they didn't linger, but silently went back to their patrol of Main Street.

That afternoon they reached a new low in cooperation. Maud had been holding the door of the supermarket open for a man who was weighed down with bags and boxes, and got her cape stuck when the door swung shut. Ernie pretended not to see. Because Maud refused to ask for his help, she had to wait there, glowering, till a kind passerby stopped to release her.

When Ernie tripped and fell outside the supermarket while trying to catch Mrs. Wilkins's runaway tomatoes, Maud didn't rush to his assistance. Instead, seeing that Ernie had fallen on the tomatoes, she just snickered unkindly and said in a funny voice that Ernie suspected was meant to mimic his own, "Super Whiz recommends heavy-duty detergent for those stubborn stains."

As the end of the day approached and the two superheroes made their way back to 32 Main Street, Ernie knew that they couldn't carry on this way. He had to do something.

"Hey, Maud?" he said casually.

She looked up in surprise. It had been nearly two hours since she gave him the laundry tip and neither of them had uttered a word in that time. "What?" she asked suspiciously.

"Why don't we grab a milkshake or something, after we've reported back to base?" Ernie suggested.

"I'm afraid I don't have time, Ernie," Maud said haughtily. "I have a lot to do before my Sidekick

Tryouts tomorrow."

Something in Ernie snapped. "Well, I hope you get a better sidekick than I've got!" he shouted.

Maud gave an outraged bleat. "What's that supposed to mean?" she demanded.

"It means that you've been so busy with your stupid sidekicks that I might as well have been patrolling on my own for the past week!" Ernie yelled.

"Are you saying that I'm selfish?" Maud shot back. "Ha! You should be called Super Selfish! But I suppose that's typical of an only child — you think you should have everything your own way!"

Ernie could feel himself swelling with rage, but before he could respond he heard a quiet, firm voice behind him. "You two! Inside at once!"

Turning, he saw Valiant Vera glaring at them from the doorway of the blank storefront that was the Baxter Branch of the Superheroes Society. "We could hear you quite clearly even with the door shut," she said severely. "And I imagine the rest of Baxter could too."

Meekly, Ernie and Maud followed Valiant Vera inside.

"This is NOT the superhero spirit," said Valiant Vera sternly, once the door had shut behind them. "As superheroes, we never argue among ourselves."

Super Whiz and Amazing Desmond both looked a little uncomfortable at this, as they had been known to bicker occasionally. But they

didn't dare contradict Valiant Vera, who sounded
almost fierce.

"I don't care who started it, or whose fault it
is," she said, holding up a hand as Ernie and Maud
began to talk at once. "Until you two can work
together, I don't want to see either of you here.

Now, go home and don't come back until this problem is sorted out!"

Ernie quaked inside. Not come back to the Superheroes Society? Being a superhero was the most important thing in the world to him! He glanced at Maud. He knew she felt the same way — surely they could work this out. But Maud refused to meet his eye. Ernie felt his anger surfacing once again. Fine!

They both headed to the door and reached it at the same time.

Ernie opened it and stood back to let Maud pass. "After you," he said coldly.

"No, thank you," said Maud. Her voice was like ice. "After you."

Ernie exited without another word and marched down Main Street toward home without a backward look.

FIVE

On Sunday morning Ernie was in low spirits. He decided to have a lazy morning in his pajamas. He was just settling himself onto the sofa with a cup of cocoa to watch a special one-hour episode of his favorite show, *The Daring Dynamo*, when he heard a tap at the door.

At first, seeing what looked like fleece through the peephole, Ernie thought it was Maud, come to apologize. But no. It was a tiny little sheep — more of a lamb, really. Her big wide eyes were framed with long dark lashes, and her fleece fell in soft white curls. A faded dish towel was pinned

around her neck. She was the cutest sheep Ernie had ever seen.

"You must be Mavis," he said.

Mavis nodded shyly. "I'm Maud's sister," she piped in a high, clear voice. "Have you seen Maud today?"

Ernie shook his head.

"I can't find her anywhere," said Mavis sadly.

"Wait!" said Ernie, as she turned away from the door. "Wasn't Maud holding her Sidekick Tryouts today?"

The little sheep looked at him hopefully.

"You could try Mackie's Meadow," Ernie suggested.

With a grateful baa, Mavis trotted away on her tiny legs.

Ernie went back to his cartoon, but his mind wasn't on the adventures of The Daring Dynamo. Instead of urging on his hero in his latest battle with Count Crustaceous, he found himself thinking of Maud. Ernie felt bad about snapping at her. He should have been more sensitive — she was obviously upset when she arrived late yesterday morning. But instead of being supportive, he had thought only of himself. Maud was right — he *was* selfish.

Then Ernie had an idea. He would go along to the Sidekick Tryouts and see if Maud needed any help. That would show her he cared.

Feeling happier already, he ran to his room and pulled on jeans and a sweater. Within ten minutes he was jogging down the road on his way to Mackie's Meadow.

He could hear the noise from several blocks away — braying, bleating, crowing, croaking — and as he approached Ernie was surprised by the size of the gathering. He noticed a donkey, several goats, two roosters, chickens, ducks, ponies, and — was that a rat?

Bustling about importantly among the crowd of animals was Maud. She was wearing her pink cape and a visor to keep the sun out of her eyes and she had a clipboard hanging from a piece of string tied around her neck, next to a whistle.

Ernie hung around at the edge of the crowd between two pigs. He was a little nervous about

what sort of welcome he might get. Finally, he plucked up his courage and called, "Maud! Over here!"

At the sound of his voice Maud turned her head and scanned the crowd. When her eyes rested on him, her face broke out into a huge sunny smile. "Ernie!" she cried, trotting over. "What are you doing here?"

"I, er, I thought you might want some help," Ernie said. He looked at the ground. "Listen,

Maud," he began, "I'm sorry about . . ."

But Maud didn't let him finish. "I'm the one who should be apologizing," she said. "I don't know what got into me. I've been acting like a sheep with a sore head. Friends?"

"Friends!" replied Ernie happily. "Now, what can I do to help?"

"Well, Ernie," said Maud, "it would be great if we could share some of our experiences with the group. You know, as an example of all the teamwork and cooperation that goes into being a superhero."

"That's a great idea, Maud," Ernie said admiringly.

Maud gave a short, sharp blast of her whistle, and there was an immediate hush. "If you'll all sit down," she called, "we'll begin by outlining the duties of a superhero team."

After a brief tussle in which the smaller animals jostled their way to the front, Ernie found himself looking into a sea of faces.

"This is my partner, Extraordinary Ernie," Maud continued, gesturing with a hoof toward the blushing Ernie.

Ernie cleared his throat and began to talk about the patrols he and Maud did up and down Main Street and around the park, offering their assistance to the people — "and animals," Maud added — of Baxter.

The crowd nodded and murmured.

"Don't forget about the time you saved me from that vicious dog," Maud said. She began to tell the story, with lots of dramatic emphasis.

The animals stared open-mouthed, hanging on her every word.

"Oh, and what about the time we helped Emma Plucker with those bullies?" Ernie reminded her.

Maud began to laugh. "That's right," she said. "Remember how you pushed one of them . . ."

"And you stood behind him, so that when he fell . . ." Ernie chimed in.

"He tumbled right into the pond!" Maud finished.

They both began to laugh.

"So you see," Maud said, "if you want to be a

good superhero sidekick, there's nothing more important than trust and teamwork."

"And a good friendship," Ernie added.

"That's right," Maud agreed, giving him a warm smile. "And a good friendship."

The next couple of hours were spent playing a series of games that Maud had invented to test qualities like speed and coordination. Ernie didn't always understand the rules — "No, Wesley," Maud explained patiently to a middle guinea pig for the third time, "you have to grip the bag with your *teeth*, or it doesn't work" — but he had a wonderful time.

After the games they all sat in a circle and, one by one, the animals introduced themselves and talked about why they wanted to be superhero sidekicks. Ernie was fascinated by some of their stories. "I never knew frogs were so ambitious," he whispered to Maud.

They finished up around mid-afternoon, and the animals began drifting off, with Maud promising to continue the tryouts the following Sunday. Ernie was helping Maud pack up her things when

he noticed a sheep cantering across the meadow. She looked a lot like Maud, but with glasses.

"Um, Maud," Ernie said, "I think Doris is here."

"What?" Maud turned to look in surprise. "It *is* Doris," she said. "I wonder what she wants." Maud trotted over to greet her older sister, followed closely by Ernie.

"Have you seen Mavis?" Doris bleated breathlessly.

"She stopped by my place this morning," Ernie said. "She was looking for Maud, so I sent her over here."

Maud's face took on a stubborn look. "She did come here," she said. "But I sent her straight home."

"When would that have been?" Doris asked.

"Oh, about three or four hours ago," replied Maud. "Why?"

Doris looked serious. "Mavis is missing," she said.

SIX

"Missing?" Maud echoed.

Doris was looking at her helplessly. "What should we do, Maud?" she asked.

Maud pulled herself together. "It's all right, Doris," she said. "You know how dreamy Mavis is. She probably wandered down to the park and has lost track of time. You go home and wait there in case she shows up. Ernie and I will go and look around the park."

As soon as Doris had left, though, Maud's face dropped. "This is all my fault," she wailed. "Mavis showed up at the tryouts this morning, but I wouldn't let her enter because she wasn't a middle child!" She sniffled, then said, "Plus I was still angry at her for taking my cape for her dress-up again yesterday. She got it all creased and crumply — and she knows how important that cape is to me!"

Ernie gave her shoulder a reassuring pat. "Don't worry, Maud," he said. "We'll find her."

Ernie and Maud took off at a run, making a quick detour to Ernie's house so he could change into his green superhero costume. Catching a glimpse of himself in his bedroom mirror, he already felt more confident and in control.

Maud was waiting outside on the sidewalk, still puffing after their run from Mackie's Meadow. Poor Maud: sheep weren't used to doing so much running. Then Ernie had an idea. "What we need is more speed, Maud," he told her.

"I know, Ernie," Maud panted. "But I don't think I can run any faster."

"That's okay; I have an idea." Ernie ran into the garage. When he emerged, he was wheeling a bike. He had a skateboard tucked under one arm

and a rope draped over the other.

Maud looked doubtful. "Maybe we should call a taxi," she said.

Ernie tied one end of the rope to the back of his bike and the other to the skateboard. "I was thinking that you could stand on the skateboard, holding the rope, and I could tow you with the bike," he explained.

"Ernie, that's a brilliant idea!" said Maud. "We'll be able to cover a lot more ground this way."

"One more thing!" Ernie dashed back to the garage and returned with two helmets. He put one on, then bent down to strap the other around Maud's woolly chin. "I outgrew this one last year," he told her, "but it should fit you."

When the helmet was secure, Maud hopped onto the skateboard and planted her hooves firmly on the narrow surface.

Ernie jumped onto his bike. "Ready?" he called.

"Ready!" Maud called back, picking up the rope.

"Here we go!" Ernie began to pedal. He could feel his cape begin to rise as they gathered speed and, glancing back, he saw that both his green cape and Maud's pink one were streaming behind them.

They reached the park in no time. Maud stepped off the skateboard and started trotting around the park in anxious circles. "Mavis!" she called. "Mavis!"

Ernie leaned his bike against a tree and ran to the far side of the park. "Mavis! Mavis!"

The sun was starting to sink in the sky when they met up by the pond.

"I don't think she's here, Maud," Ernie said. "And we didn't see her when we approached the park from that side," he pointed back in the direction from which they'd come, "so let's walk up Main Street and see if we can spot her."

"Okay," Maud agreed.

"In fact, why don't we report in to HQ? We can leave the bike and skateboard there, and ask the superheroes for their help."

❁

On reaching 32 Main Street, they found the superheroes gathered around the table — except Housecat Woman, who was dozing quietly in her armchair. Super Whiz had all thirteen lectures arranged on the table in front of him and was quizzing his colleagues about which one they liked best.

Ernie propped the bike against the wall while Maud hurriedly told the superheroes about her

missing sister.

"Leave her alone and she'll come home," Super Whiz advised, looking a bit irritated at the interruption.

But Amazing Desmond jumped up. "Of course we'll help," he said. "Won't we, Vera?"

"Definitely," said Valiant Vera. "And I'm glad to see you two behaving like a team again," she added.

In the end, all four superheroes — even Housecat Woman — said they'd help.

"Ahem. In times of trouble, we must rush to the aid of our superhero friends," Super Whiz stated.

No sooner had they trooped out through the shabby brown door of the Superheroes Society (Baxter Branch) than they were hailed by a man who was running down Main Street toward them.

"Come quick! There's a poor little sheep stuck in a tree!" he shouted. Then he added, "And it's the cutest sheep I've ever seen . . ."

Oh no! Mavis! The superheroes began to run.

SEVEN

Ernie and Maud were the first to reach the tree outside the supermarket. But this time, when Ernie peered up into the leaves, it wasn't a ball of fluff he saw clinging to the uppermost branches. Instead, he saw a very frightened ball of wool.

The spectators were gaping at the astonishing sight.

"Her fleece is white as snow!" exclaimed one woman in wonder.

"Mavis!" cried Maud urgently, as Valiant Vera, Housecat Woman, and Super Whiz approached the scene. "Is that you?"

"Maud," bleated Mavis pathetically from the top of the tree. She began to cry.

"Don't worry, Mavis," said Maud. "We'll get you down — won't we, Ernie?"

"Yeah!" said Ernie, trying to sound confident. He turned to Maud. "I'm sorry, Maud," he said in a whisper, "but I don't think I can climb down a tree carrying a sheep!"

The superheroes began a hushed conversation.

"How are we going to get her down?" Maud asked in despair.

"The question is how she got up there in the first place," Super Whiz said.

Valiant Vera shushed him. "That's not important now," she said, looking up at the trembling lamb. "What I'm most worried about is Mavis slipping. I imagine that it's hard to grip with hooves."

Maud nodded fearfully.

"Yes, yes," said Super Whiz loudly. "Our first action must be to secure the sheep to the branch. So, any ideas?" He looked around the circle.

"Um, I've got one," said Ernie. "Housecat Woman, I bet you're a fantastic climber."

"That's true," said Housecat Woman. "I used to do a lot of climbing as a kitt — er, kid."

"Could you climb up the tree with a rope and tie Mavis to the branch so she doesn't fall?"

"Easy," said Housecat Woman, looking more alert than Ernie had ever seen her. "Give me the rope."

The superheroes looked at each other. "All

right," said Super Whiz bossily. "We've estab-
lished that we need a rope urgently. Desmond,
you're good at finding things in a flash . . .
Desmond?"

But Amazing Desmond was nowhere to be
seen.

"That Desmond!" said Super Whiz, stamping
his foot. "He always disappears right when you
need him most."

"That's not really fair . . ." Valiant Vera began.

"I used a rope to tie the skateboard to the
bike!" Ernie interrupted. "I'll run and get it."

He dashed back down Main Street to the
Superheroes Society and within a couple of minutes was racing back up to where the superheroes
were gathered around the tree.

"Good work, Ernie," said Valiant Vera as he
handed the rope to Housecat Woman. She im-
mediately coiled the rope around her shoulder
and began scaling the trunk.

"I'm scared, Maud," bleated Mavis from the
top of the tree, wobbling dangerously.

The onlookers and superheroes gasped.

"Please hang on, Mavis," Maud called. "House-cat Woman is on her way up with a rope. She'll tie you to the tree so you don't fall."

To the relief of all below, the words had barely left Maud's lips before Housecat Woman could be seen busily securing the little sheep to the branch.

"That's one problem taken care of," said Valiant Vera. "But we still haven't solved the big problem. How on earth are we going to get Mavis down?"

Super Whiz, meanwhile, was still fuming about Desmond. "Here we are, in the middle of a crisis, and where's Desmond?"

His fuming was interrupted by the sound of an enormous engine. Rumbling down the street was a giant crane — and there, waving from the driver's seat, was Amazing Desmond.

"Looking for me, Whiz?" he cried.

"What? Where? Why?" stammered Super Whiz.

"It's a crane, obviously," said Desmond. "And I borrowed it from the building site down the

street. I thought we could use it to hoist Mavis out of the tree. Or do you have a better idea?"

The other superheroes silently shook their heads.

"Okay, then," said Desmond. "What next?"

"Well, we've already got a rope in place," Maud said. "We could just take the end of rope that's tied around the tree and attach it to the crane instead."

They all looked around for Housecat Woman.

"There she is!" cried Ernie, pointing.

Housecat Woman, exhausted from her climb, was stretched along a lower branch of the tree, fast asleep.

"There'll be no waking her now," said Valiant Vera with a sigh.

"I'll go," Ernie offered. "I'm not as fast as Housecat Woman, but I know I can do it."

Maud positioned herself beneath the bottom branch and Ernie stepped lightly onto her back. "Watch out for the crumbly bark, Ernie," she reminded him.

Taking extra care not to slip, Ernie slowly and carefully climbed the tree.

"Hi there, Mavis," he said, when at last he reached the highest branch.

"Hi, Ernie," Mavis said in a small voice. "Have you come to save me?"

"We'll have you down in two shakes of a lamb's tail," promised Ernie with a smile.

Mavis giggled weakly.

"I'm going to tie one end of this rope to the

crane and fasten the other end
around your waist — er, your
middle," he explained, as Desmond
moved the tip of the crane till
it was within Ernie's reach.
"Amazing Desmond will lower
you down to the ground."

Ernie quickly tied the
rope in place and tugged the knots
to make sure they were tight. Then he gave Desmond the thumbs-up, and Mavis began to rise
from the branch. Swinging slightly, her dish towel fluttering in the breeze, she was soon clear of
the tree's branches and being lowered slowly to
earth.

As Ernie clambered down the tree, he could
hear the applause of the relieved crowd.

A few minutes later, Ernie joined Maud, who
was awaiting her sister's arrival on the ground.
They could just hear a high-pitched bleat.

"What's that she's saying?" Ernie asked curi-
ously, straining his ears.

Maud rolled her eyes. "She's saying, 'Wheeee!'"

When Mavis hit the pavement with a slight bump, Maud rushed over, nimbly undoing the rope with her teeth. "Oh, Mavis," she said, nuzzling her affectionately. "What a silly little lamb you are."

Mavis wriggled impatiently, then began skipping around in happy circles. "It was just like flying, Maud!" said the little sheep, her eyes shining. "And did you see how high I was? I bet no sheep has ever gone so high!"

Maud butted her sharply. "You thank everyone for saving you, Mavis," she said sternly.

After Mavis had delivered a series of breathless thank yous, to which Maud added her own heartfelt thanks, the two sheep trotted off down the street.

While Amazing Desmond returned the crane, Ernie walked with the other superheroes back to 32 Main Street and collected his bike. Mavis might be the cutest sheep he had ever seen, he thought as he pedaled slowly through the park, but little sisters were hard work.

EIGHT

When Ernie arrived at the Superheroes Society (Baxter Branch) the following afternoon, he was pleased to find that Maud was standing outside waiting for him, her cape crisp and neat and her face cheerful.

"How's Mavis?" Ernie asked.

Maud gave a sigh. "She's fine. Still talking about how she 'flew.' I don't have the heart to be cross with her, though. Apparently the reason she kept taking my cape for her dress-up was that she was pretending to be a superhero like me."

"That would explain the dish towel," Ernie said.

"Doris says I should be flattered."

"Well, Mavis must really admire you," Ernie said. "Anyway, have you decided on a sidekick? I thought that brown duck, Samantha, was pretty good."

"No, Ernie," said Maud. "I've decided that I don't need a sidekick. But the other middle animals and I are planning to have regular get-togethers. You're invited too . . ." she added, as Ernie opened the battered brown door, ". . . as an honorary middle animal."

Ernie was touched.

Inside, they found the superheroes gathered around the table in preparation for another of Super Whiz's informative lectures. Valiant Vera smiled warmly at Ernie and Maud, and Amazing Desmond gave the pair a big wink. Housecat Woman was deep in her usual slumber.

"Ahem," said Super Whiz, clearing his throat. "This afternoon I'd like to try out a new lecture I've written for the Superheroes Conference."

"Aw, come on, Whiz," Desmond groaned loudly. "Not another one. I thought we'd agreed on 'Seventeen Strategies for Successful Super-heroing.'"

"Well, Desmond," said Super Whiz with a furious glare (he hated being called Whiz), "I think I've really hit the mark with this new paper. Even you might appreciate it."

"All right," said Desmond. "Go on then."

"Although crime is at an all-time low in Baxter, we are never short of action. Far from it . . ."

As Super Whiz began to speak, Ernie and Maud exchanged small smiles. Even if Super Whiz's lectures were a bit boring sometimes, Ernie didn't mind.

"'But how did the sheep get in the tree?' I heard someone ask. 'Colleagues,' I said, 'that is of little import in the present crisis. It is imperative that before another step is taken we first secure the sheep to the tree.'"

"Huh?" Ernie looked up, startled. Valiant Vera, with a puzzled expression on her face, looked as if she was about to say something, but Super Whiz carried on.

"'Fellow superheroes,' I said, 'it is a crane

we seek.'"

Amazing Desmond snorted loudly, but Super Whiz continued as if there had been no interruption.

This wasn't quite the way Ernie remembered things happening, but as he settled back to listen he had to admit it was a gripping story.

"And so, the sheep was borne safely to earth. And a very cute sheep she was, too."

All the superheroes gathered around Super

Whiz, clapping and cheering. Although he may have muddled up a few of the details, he had certainly made the rescue of Mavis sound like a very exciting adventure. They all agreed that this was by far Super Whiz's best lecture ever.

About the author

Fearless Frances Watts is the author of *Kisses for Daddy* and *Parsley Rabbit's Book about Books*. She also works as an editor, and as the servant of a lazy cat. Frances likes traveling, cheese, and ducks, and dislikes ferocious dogs and having cold feet. Although her natural superpower has not yet emerged, she did once rescue a horse from a fire.

About the illustrator

Jittery Judy Watson has been a chicken all her life. She has illustrated several books for children, some of them quite terrifying. Her most frightening project so far was drawing the fearsome tiger for the Aussie Nibble *Tim & Tig*. Drawing the pictures for *Extraordinary Ernie & Marvelous Maud* sometimes caused her hand to tremble. This may explain many of the wobbles in her illustrations.

By the way, she is very impressed that Fearless Frances has rescued a horse.

Ernie & Maud

Also available

Extraordinary Ernie & Marvelous Maud

Ernie Eggers is thrilled when he wins a superhero contest and becomes Extraordinary Ernie (after school on Mondays, Tuesdays, and Thursdays, and all day Saturday). But his excitement turns to dismay when he discovers that his sidekick is a sheep. It doesn't take him long to realize, though, that there has never been another sheep quite like Marvelous Maud.

Coming soon

The Greatest Sheep in History

Extraordinary Ernie and Marvelous Maud are back!

Ernie and Maud are thrilled to be attending the National Superheroes Conference with the other superheroes from Baxter. But when the conference is disrupted by Chicken George — the most terrifying and villainous chicken anyone has ever seen — it will take more than just an ordinary superhero to save the day.